To my father, Emilio: He gave me firm roots and strong branches that have enveloped me for a lifetime.

Lorenza

To Lamberto, great tree, great father, who has been able to protect me with his fronds and that I will never forget…when he lost all his leaves.

Manuela

Copyright © FIGLIE DI SAN PAOLO, 2019 with the title *Il Guerriero di Legno* by Lorenza Farina, Illustrations by Manuela Simoncelli; English translation copyright © 2021 by Paulist Press.

All rights reserved. No part of this publication may be reproduced, stored in a retrieval system, or transmitted in any form or by any means, electronic, mechanical, photocopying, recording, scanning, or otherwise, without either the prior written permission of the Publisher, or authorization through payment of the appropriate per-copy fee to the Copyright Clearance Center, Inc., www.copyright.com. Requests to the Publisher for permission should be addressed to the Permissions Department, Paulist Press, permissions@paulistpress.com.

Library of Congress Control Number: 2021933121

ISBN 978-0-8091-6796-8 (hardcover)
ISBN 978-1-58768-936-9 (e-book)

PAOLINE Editoriale Libri
via Francesco Albani, 21
20149 Milan – Italy

Published by Paulist Press
997 Macarthur Boulevard
Mahwah, New Jersey 07430
www.paulistpress.com

Printed and bound in the
United States of America
by Corporate Graphics Commercial
North Mankato, MN
March 2021

LORENZA FARINA

How Grandfather Tree Forgot His Stories

Illustrated by
Manuela Simoncelli

Paulist Press
New York / Mahwah, NJ

Once upon a time in the Deep Forest, there stood a tree with splendid dark green leaves. Its slender, straight trunk soared toward the sky.

 This tall, proud tree was Grandfather Tree. Ever since he was a young sapling, Grandfather Tree had been a storyteller, from sunrise to sunset, and even at night.

Stories came from his dark green leafy top like lively rabbits from a magician's hat and hovered over that forest. Impatient stories often fought among themselves to get out first from the tangle of branches.

The trees in the forest, especially the younger ones, loved Grandfather Tree's stories. On starry nights, they called out to each other to gather around. Without moving a twig or even a tiny leaf, they listened in silence to the warm, deep voice of Grandfather Tree.

Not only trees, but also animals of the forest, and the sun, moon, wind, and rainbow wanted to hear at least one of those wonderful stories. Grandfather Tree told his tales, sometimes sad and sometimes cheerful, with such great storytelling that everyone was amazed.

"Grandfather Tree, can you tell me a short story in rhyming sentences?" Birchtree asked, his eyes sparkling with excitement.

"Once upon a time, there was a king who wanted to drink only tea…

but his queen would serve only coffee, so terribly…" he began.

The Oak trees liked to hear stories about tasty food, so Grandfather Tree dished out stories seasoned with tomato and basil, garlic, oil, and chili.

"Grandfather Tree, do you know a story about fear?" Owl asked him, feathers quivering.

Out came a story full of witches, werewolves, and vampires doing scary things on a dark and stormy night.

Squirrel loved the crunchy stories that were like eating hazelnuts. Crow demanded only stories in black and white. Rainbow preferred them in all colors and exciting like fireworks.

"Grandfather Tree, would you tell me a lullaby?"
Full Moon asked before going to bed,
for otherwise he could not sleep.

The patient old tree rummaged through its
matted hair and pulled out a brand-new lullaby,
sweet and tender as a cream-filled donut.

Sun burned brightly when he heard stories about hot summers and diving into the sea.

Wind did not know how to resist cheerful stories and jokes that crackled like popcorn popping over a fire.

Every day and every night, Grandfather Tree told stories until his voice became quiet as a whisper.

The winds blew over seasons and over years, and Grandfather Tree grew older and older.

Summer ended. And autumn passed, leaving behind a trail of leaves. Then Frosty Winter looked out with sharp gusts of north wind, sweeping away leaves, shaking tree branches, and pulling up tender shrubs.

One dark night during a very cold winter, Grandfather Tree suddenly forgot his stories. He could not remember a single one, not even the shortest story. When Grandfather Tree forgot his stories, he also lost his voice, except for one rattling sound in his knotted trunk.

Since he had survived so many storms, Grandfather Tree now felt like a plant without roots, wrapped in dark silence. It shook him deep inside.

No one noticed during that winter because all the animals of the forest were tucked away for the long cold days and nights.

Trees wrapped themselves tightly in their bark, folding their branches around their trunks to keep away the frost.

Spring finally arrived.

Birds chirped again and nature woke up. Animals came out of their winter hiding places.

"Grandfather Tree, tell us a story," the younger trees invited him over and over again.

But the old tree did not respond. He did not seem to know who anyone was anymore.

To wake him up, the younger trees, one by one, began telling him the stories he had told them for so many years without ever getting tired.

It was then that their tree buds sprouted the first leaves on which the stories of Grandfather Tree were written in the language of the trees.

The wind could not tear away those leaves, written like so many pages of a book.

The scorching summer sun did not make them fade.

And autumn rains did not erase a single word.

Every moonlit night, the younger trees read to older trees the stories hanging from their branches—a Forest of Words that Grandfather Tree had passed on to them.

A light breeze caressed their leafy tops.

Grandfather Tree listened to those stories in silence, as if he had never heard them before.

His wrinkled face looked like stone. But his sturdy heart kept beating to the rhythm of those stories that would live forever. They were words and stories in which Grandfather Tree left a part of himself.